FORMULA 1: ZOOM! ZOOM!

ALL ABOUT FORMULA ONE RACING FOR KIDS

Children's Cars & Trucks

Left Brain Kids

Educational Books for Children

LET'S TALK ABOUT ONE OF
THE STUNNING PRODUCTS OF
THE TECHNOLOGICAL WORLD—
THE FORMULA 1 RACE CAR.

WHAT DO YOU KNOW ABOUT FORMULA ONE RACING?

Perhaps, you've seen a race on television or in photos. Welcome to the world's fastest motor sport!

Formula 1 is the most technologically advanced auto racing in the world. Racers find it competitive and often dangerous. Its major races are known as Grand Prix.

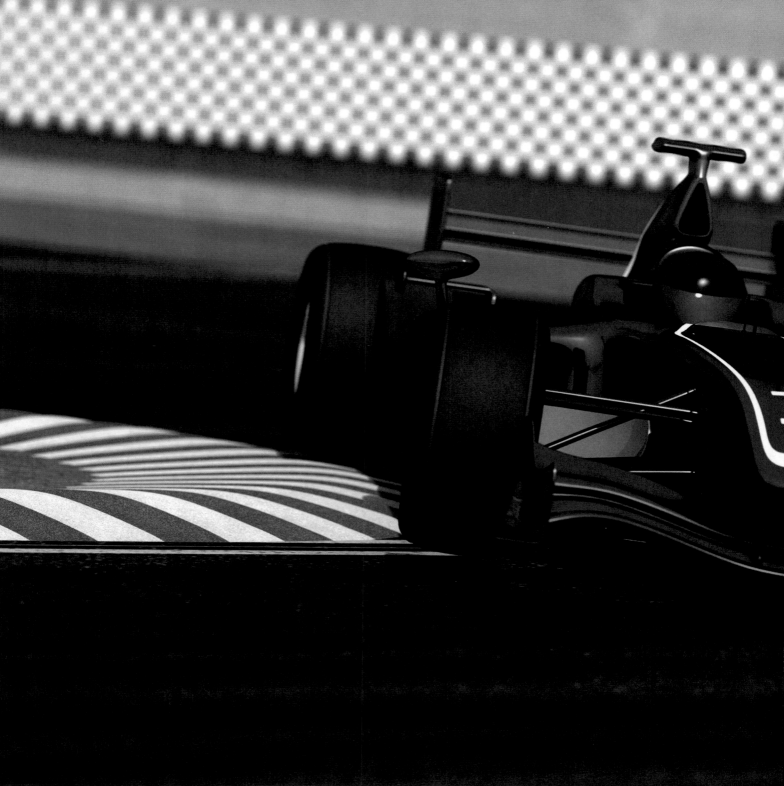

Formula 1 is the most advanced competition for drivers and cars. It is a stunning rivalry between teams of cars. One needs discipline, money and expert knowledge to build a car and join in the race.

Formula 1 automobile racing can be traced back to European Grand Pix Motor Racing in the 1920s.

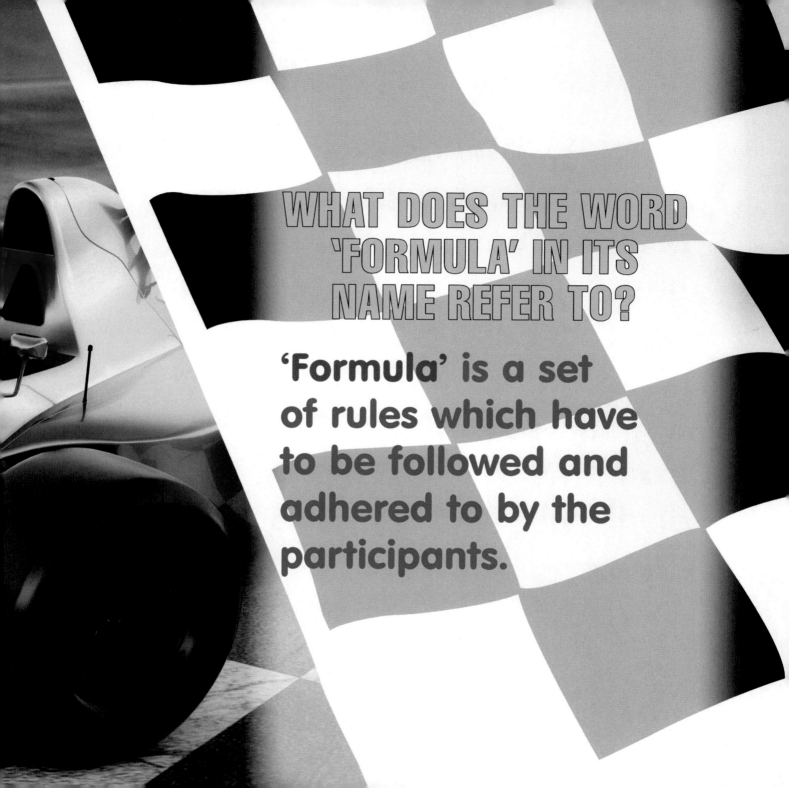

WHAT DOES THE WORD 'FORMULA' IN ITS NAME REFER TO?

'Formula' is a set of rules which have to be followed and adhered to by the participants.

Formula 1, or "F1", is very expensive. Its price may make your head spin. The cost to run a car for a season of racing may be $6 to 8 million, or more! This excludes the cost of designing and building the car. It is really a pricey machine.

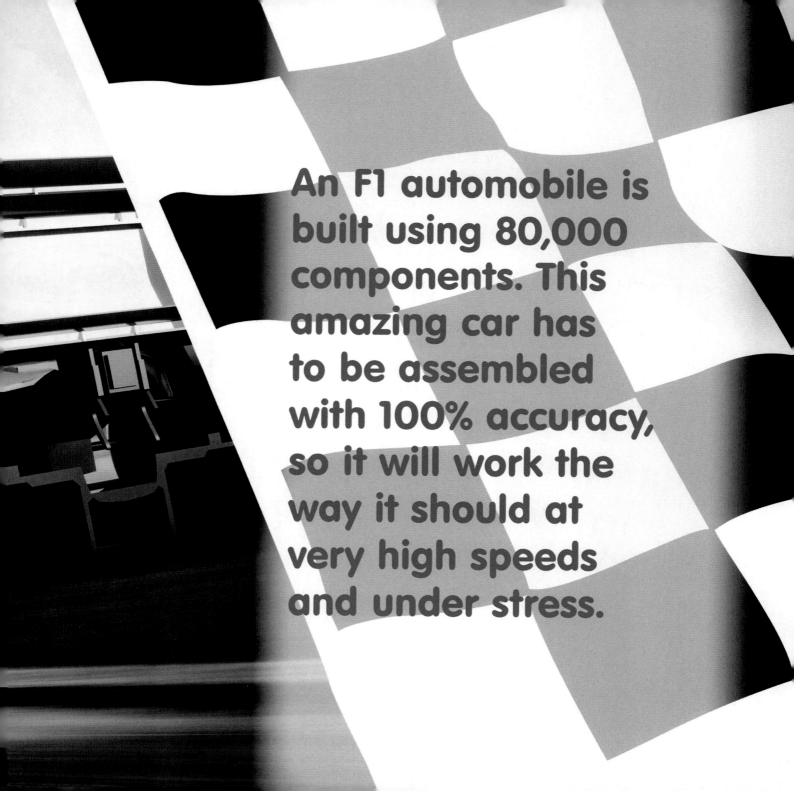

An F1 automobile is built using 80,000 components. This amazing car has to be assembled with 100% accuracy, so it will work the way it should at very high speeds and under stress.

It can accelerate from 0 to 160 kph, or decelerate back to 0, in 4 seconds. This sounds really fantastic. Formula 1 car racing is amazing.

In just one race, the driver can lose 4 kg of his weight, mainly through sweat.
The F1 automobile is equipped with a cockpit with drinking bottles for the drivers.

Drivers can drink the water hands-free, by using a tube. Not only do the drivers lose weight during the race, but also the tires!

Due to wear, each of the tires loses 0.5kg in weight. The tires of the F1 only last up to 120 km of racing.

An F1 car, including the driver, can weigh up to 702 kg. F1 cars are refueled at 12 liters per second.

An F1 pit stop crew can refuel the car and change its tires in only 3 seconds. Yes, as quick as that!

F1 car engines are known to be among the most complex products of engineering one can imagine.

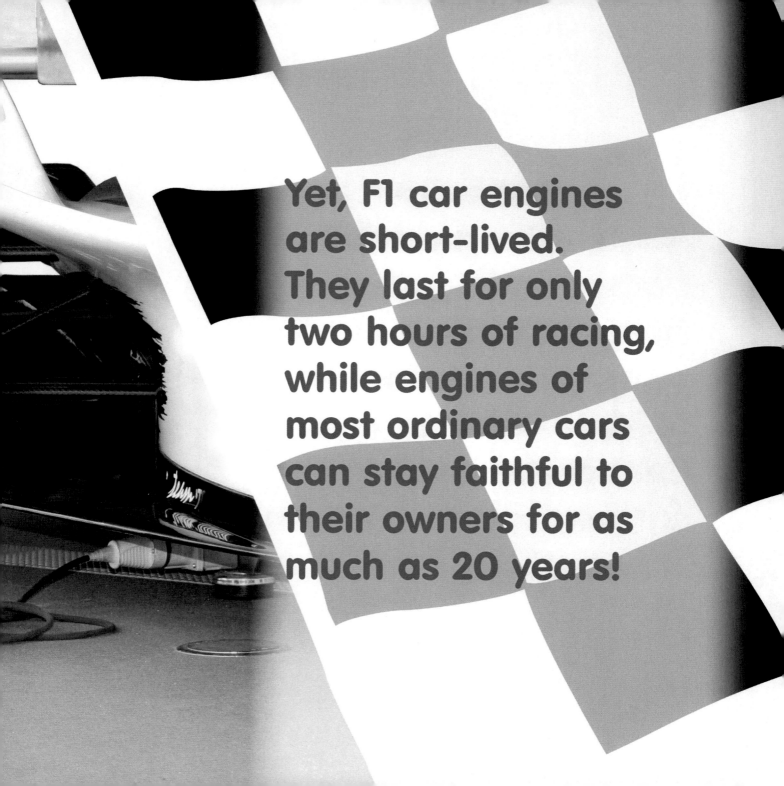

Yet, F1 car engines are short-lived. They last for only two hours of racing, while engines of most ordinary cars can stay faithful to their owners for as much as 20 years!

F1 car brake discs, made of carbon fiber, are designed to withstand temperatures up to 1000 degrees Centigrade. The carbon fiber is much harder than steel.

The F1 car is really amazing, with its top speed of 360 kilometers per hour.

F1 drivers have to be physically fit to withstand stresses from accelerating and the possibility of crash impacts during the race. They have to be as tough as their helmets are.

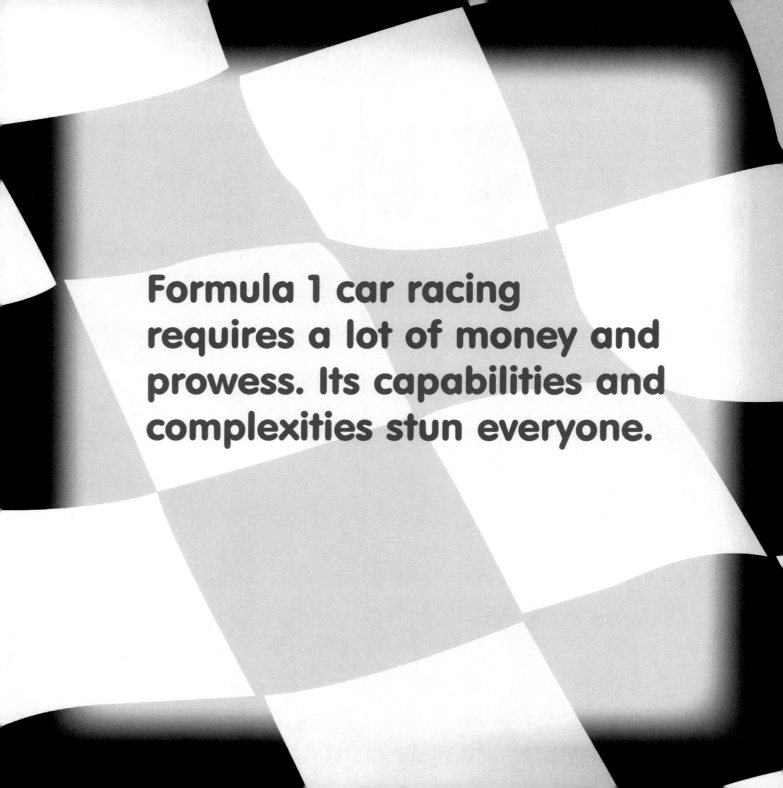

Formula 1 car racing requires a lot of money and prowess. Its capabilities and complexities stun everyone.

It's most advanced features are astonishing. F1 automobile racing is really impressive!

Made in the USA
Las Vegas, NV
06 December 2023